SPOTLIGHT ON PHYSICAL SCIENCE

GRAVITATIONAL, MAGNETIC, AND ELECTRIC FORCES

EXAMINING INTERACTIONS

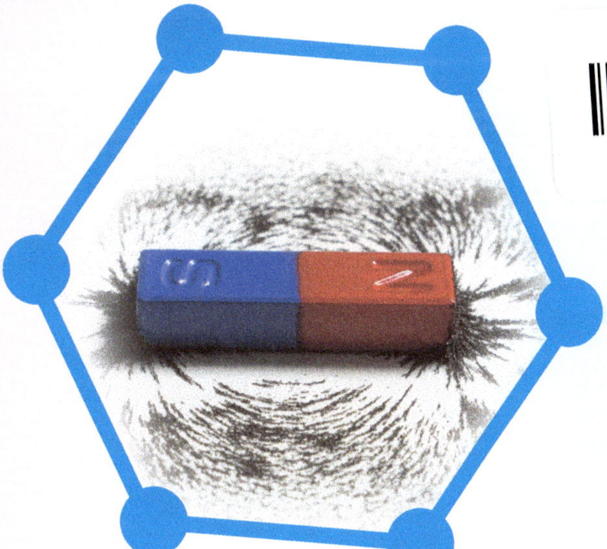

DANIEL R. FAUST

PowerKiDS press.
NEW YORK

Published in 2020 by The Rosen Publishing Group, Inc.
29 East 21st Street, New York, NY 10010

Editor: Elizabeth Krajnik
Book Design: Michael Flynn

Photo Credits: Cover, p. 1 ShutterStockStudio/Shutterstock.com; (series molecular background) pro500/Shutterstock.com; p. 5 Christi Tolbert/Shutterstock.com; p. 6 vnlit/Shutterstock.com; p. 7 leeborn/Shutterstock.com; p. 9 (main) Georgios Kollidas/Shutterstock.com; p. 9 (inset) https://commons.wikimedia.org/wiki/File:NewtonsPrincipia.jpg; p. 10 Transcendental Graphics/Archive Photos/Getty Images; p. 11 Julia Kopacheva/Shutterstock.com; p. 13 YummyBuum/Shutterstock.com; p. 14 https://commons.wikimedia.org/wiki/File:Black_hole_-_Messier_87.jpg; p. 15 paulista/Shutterstock.com; p. 16 haryigit/Shutterstock.com; p. 17 dvande/Shutterstock.com; p. 18 Vector FX/Shutterstock.com; p. 19 https://commons.wikimedia.org/wiki/File:Charles_de_Coulomb.png; p. 20 Kryuchka Yaroslav/Shutterstock.com; p. 21 Karyna Che/Shutterstock.com; p. 23 John D Sirlin/Shutterstock.com; p. 24 Craig Walton/Shutterstock.com; p. 25 nerosu/Shutterstock.com; p. 26 Mopic/Shutterstock.com; p. 27 Naeblys/Shutterstock.com; p. 29 Ash T productions/Shutterstock.com.

Cataloging-in-Publication Data

Names: Faust, Daniel R.
Title: Gravitational, magnetic, & electric forces: examining interactions / Daniel R. Faust.
Description: New York : PowerKids Press, 2020. | Series: Spotlight on physical science | Includes glossary and index.
Identifiers: ISBN 9781725313095 (pbk.) | ISBN 9781725313125 (library bound) | ISBN 9781725313101 (6 pack)
Subjects: LCSH: Gravity--Juvenile literature. | Electromagnetism--Juvenile literature. | Magnetism--Juvenile literature.
Classification: LCC QB334.F38 2020 | DDC 530--dc23

Manufactured in the United States of America

CPSIA Compliance Information: Batch #CWPK20. For further information contact Rosen Publishing, New York, New York at 1-800-237-9932.

CONTENTS

CHAPTER ONE

THE FOUR FUNDAMENTAL FORCES

Why does your pen fall to the floor when it rolls off the desk? How does flipping a light switch turn the lights in your house on and off? How can a compass help you find your way? These things and many more are all because of the four **fundamental** forces of nature. A force is a push or pull that changes an object's motion or causes it to change shape. Forces are acting on us all the time.

One of the four fundamental forces is gravity. Gravity is the force that pulls you and everything around you towards Earth's center. Another force is electromagnetic force. This includes both electric and magnetic forces because they have the same underlying cause. The other two forces—the strong force and the weak force—work at the atomic level, which makes it hard for us to see them in action.

If you throw a ball and no one catches it, the ball will fall to the ground. Gravity makes that happen.

CHAPTER TWO

WHAT IS GRAVITY?

Gravity is probably the first force you learned about. When you were learning to walk, gravity pulled you to the ground when you fell. It's also the force that pulls a leaf to the ground when it falls from a tree.

Earth's gravitational force is also responsible for Earth's atmosphere. Without Earth's powerful gravitational pull, all the oxygen and other gases we need to survive would float into space.

Gravity is a force that draws two objects to each other. Gravity acts upon all things with mass. Everything on Earth has mass. The greater an object's mass, the greater its gravity. The relationship between mass and gravity is what makes life on Earth possible. The rocks, trees, water, and living things on Earth's surface are held there by Earth's gravitational force. Their mass is far smaller than Earth's mass, which is what keeps them from flying off into space. Gravity is also what keeps the planets in orbit around the sun, because the sun's mass is far greater than the mass of any of the planets.

CHAPTER THREE

NEWTON AND EINSTEIN

Two scientists did much of the work to provide us with knowledge about gravity and how it acts upon objects: Sir Isaac Newton and Albert Einstein. Newton was a 17th-century English mathematician, **physicist**, and astronomer. He was known as a natural philosopher, or a person who studied nature and the physical world in the days before the modern sciences.

In 1687's *Philosophiae Naturalis Principia Mathematica*, known simply as *Principia*, Newton wrote about the laws of motion and universal gravitation that became the main scientific theory for more than 200 years. Newton's theories helped prove Johannes Kepler's laws of planetary motion. They also helped prove that the sun was the center of the solar system. Newton's work also helped explain the interaction between celestial bodies such as planets and moons and accounted for the motion of the tides of Earth's oceans.

Philosophiae Naturalis Principia Mathematica, which means *Mathematical Principles of Natural Philosophy* in Latin, is considered Newton's masterpiece, as well as one of the most important works of modern science.

SIR ISAAC NEWTON

PHILOSOPHIÆ
NATURALIS
PRINCIPIA
MATHEMATICA.

Autore JS. NEWTON, Trin. Coll. Cantab. Soc. Matheseos Professore Lucasiano, & Societatis Regalis Sodali.

IMPRIMATUR.
S. PEPYS, Reg. Soc. PRÆSES.
Julii 5. 1686.

LONDINI,
Jussu Societatis Regiæ ac Typis Josephi Streater. Prostat apud plures Bibliopolas. Anno MDCLXXXVII.

In 1905, physicist Albert Einstein published two theories that would greatly change what we know about gravity and the universe. The first theory is known as the special theory of relativity. This theory explained that the laws of physics are the same for all observers going the same constant speed. It explained that space and time are connected.

ALBERT EINSTEIN

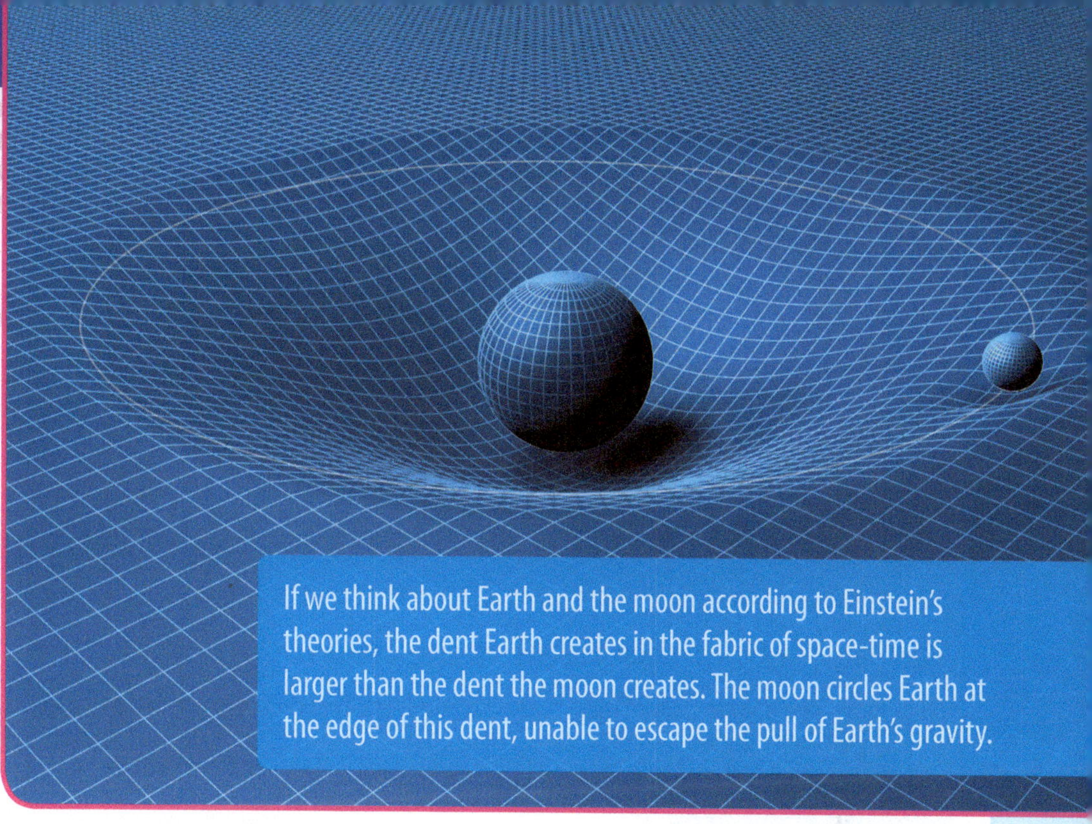

If we think about Earth and the moon according to Einstein's theories, the dent Earth creates in the fabric of space-time is larger than the dent the moon creates. The moon circles Earth at the edge of this dent, unable to escape the pull of Earth's gravity.

Ten years later, Einstein developed the second theory, the general theory of relativity. This theory made some changes to Newton's laws of motion to account for fast-moving and extremely large objects. According to Einstein, **space-time** can be **distorted** by massive objects, such stars and planets, creating gravitational pull. Imagine space-time is a trampoline. Placing a heavy object, like a bowling ball, on the trampoline creates a dent in the fabric. A smaller object, like a marble, could get caught in that dent and fall towards the bowling ball.

CHAPTER FOUR

GRAVITY, MASS, AND WEIGHT

Many people use the words "mass" and "weight" as if they mean the same thing. In reality, even though the two terms are related, they mean different things. Mass is a measurement of how much matter is in an object. Weight, on the other hand, is the measurement of how much gravitational force is working upon an object.

Mass is a constant, meaning an object's mass remains the same no matter where the object is located. Weight, however, can change. If there's more gravitational force working upon an object, its weight increases. For example, if something weighs 100 pounds (45.4 kg) on Earth, it's because of the gravitational pull generated by Earth's mass. The moon has less mass than Earth, so that same object would weigh less, about 16.5 pounds (7.5 kg). The weight of an object on the moon is 16.5 percent of what it is on Earth.

Jupiter has more mass than Earth. Can you figure out how much a 100-pound (45.4 kg) object would weigh on Jupiter (2.528 times more)? The stronger the gravity, the more something weighs.

A 100-POUND (45.4 KG) OBJECT ON EARTH WOULD WEIGH . . .

107 POUNDS (48.5 KG) ON SATURN

? POUNDS (? KG) ON JUPITER

38 POUNDS (17.2 KG) ON MARS

91 POUNDS (41.3 KG) ON VENUS

38 POUNDS (17.2 KG) ON MERCURY

91 POUNDS (41.3 KG) ON URANUS

114 POUNDS (51.7 KG) ON NEPTUNE

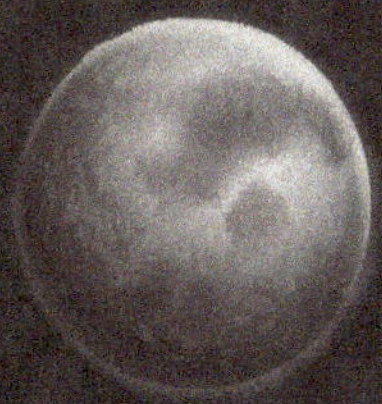

17 POUNDS (7.7 KG) ON THE MOON

CHAPTER FIVE

EXOPLANETS AND WOBBLY STARS

Astronomers are on a constant search for exoplanets, or planets that exist outside the boundaries of our own solar system. While it's easy to see distant stars from Earth because they **emit** bright light, it isn't always easy to locate other objects, such as planets. One way to locate new planets is to search for stars that appear to wobble.

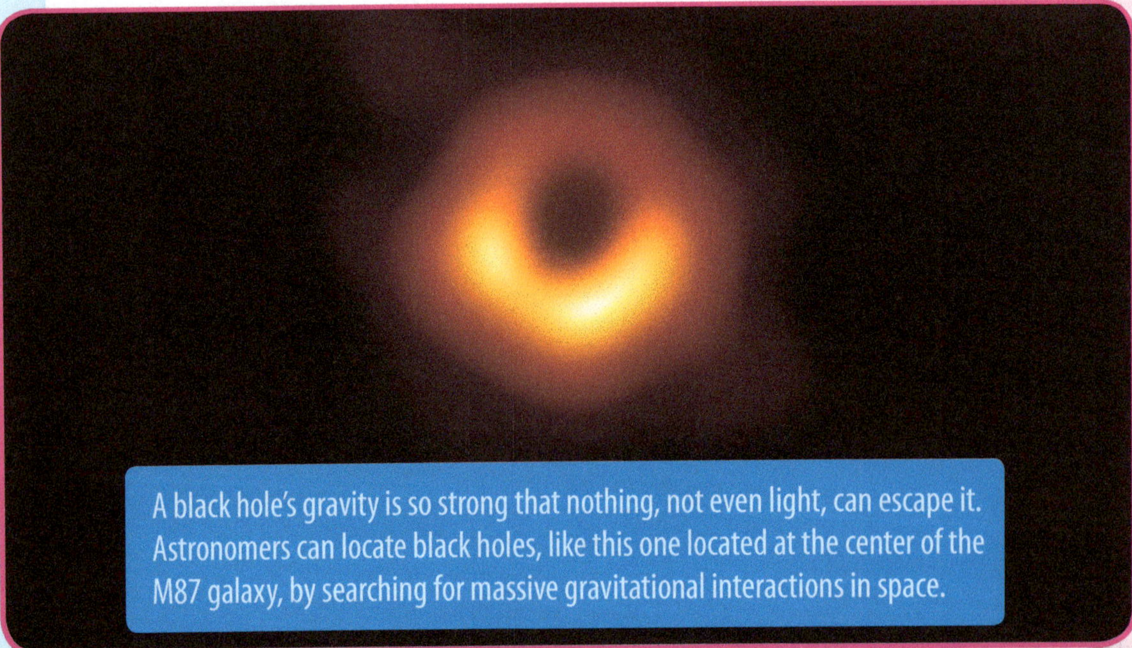

A black hole's gravity is so strong that nothing, not even light, can escape it. Astronomers can locate black holes, like this one located at the center of the M87 galaxy, by searching for massive gravitational interactions in space.

Gravity is like a game of tug-of-war between a star and a planet. The star has more mass, so it has a greater gravitational pull on the planet. However, the planet still has an effect on the star. The planet's gravitational pull on the star might be very weak, but it can still cause the star to wobble. When astronomers see this wobble, they know that there's a planet orbiting that star. The greater the wobble, the larger the planet.

CHAPTER SIX

WHAT IS THE ELECTROMAGNETIC FORCE?

The electromagnetic force is also one that we encounter every day of our lives. The electromagnetic force is an interaction that takes place between electrically charged **particles**. As we can tell from the name, the electromagnetic force has two **components**: electricity and magnetism. For a long time, scientists believed electricity and magnetism were separate forces. It wasn't until the 19th century that electricity and magnetism were treated as related forces. Einstein's special theory of relativity proved them to be part of one force.

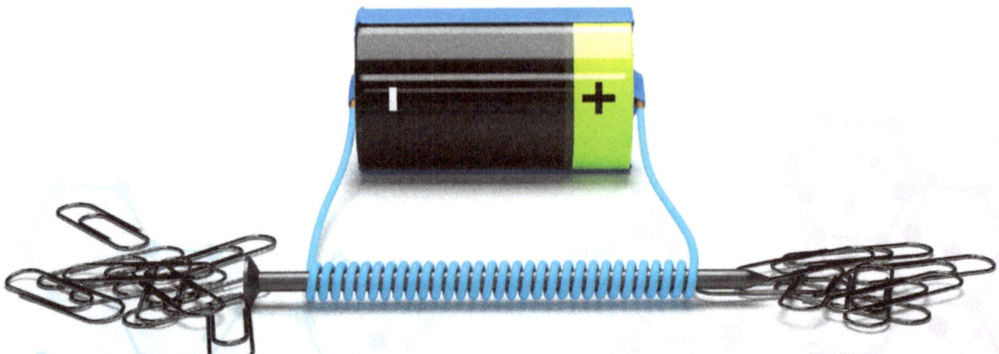

You can make a simple electromagnet at home using a battery, some wire, and an iron nail. This electromagnet operates under the same principles as giant electromagnets, such as those used to move scrap metal in junkyards.

Electrical and magnetic interactions rely on the electrically charged particles that make up all matter. The flow of electricity can generate magnetism, and magnetism can generate electricity. Coiling a wire around an iron nail and then connecting it to a battery will turn that nail into a magnet. Likewise, moving a magnet around a coiled wire will cause electricity to flow through the wire.

CHAPTER SEVEN

POSITIVE OR NEGATIVE?

Electricity is the form of energy created by electric charge. An electric charge can be positive or **negative**. This charge is carried by atomic particles called protons and electrons. Protons always carry a positive charge and electrons always carry a negative charge. The interaction between these two particles is what generates electricity.

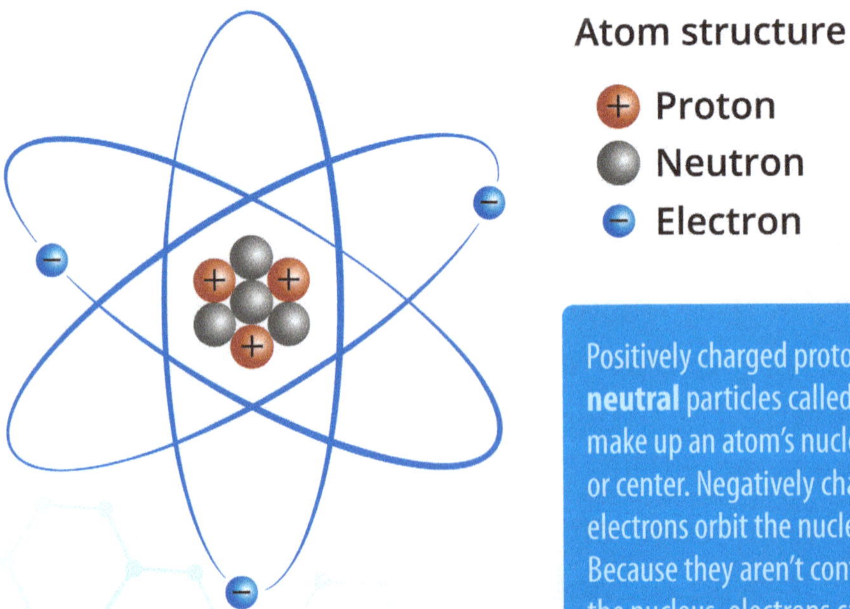

Positively charged protons and **neutral** particles called neutrons make up an atom's nucleus, or center. Negatively charged electrons orbit the nucleus. Because they aren't contained in the nucleus, electrons can break away from an atom.

CHARLES-AUGUSTIN DE COULOMB

According to Coulomb's law, named after French physicist Charles-Augustin de Coulomb, charges of the same type **repel** each other and charges of the opposite type attract each other. This is electrostatic force. This means that electrons push other electrons away. When this happens, electrons may "jump" from one atom to another, creating a chain reaction that we call electric current. Electric current is what makes it possible for us to use electricity to power our lights, televisions, computers, and smartphones.

CHAPTER EIGHT

CIRCUITS

How do we harness an electric current and use it to power our devices and appliances? To do that, we need a circuit. Circuits use wires to carry electric current to the various parts of an electrical system. Think about turning on a flashlight. When you switch on the flashlight, it completes a circuit, allowing the electric current to flow to the light bulb and turn it on.

An insulator is a material that blocks the flow of electricity. Rubber is a good insulator. The electric wires in your home may be coated in a layer of rubber to prevent you from accidentally getting hurt.

In order for a circuit to work, it needs a power source, usually a battery or generator. The power source produces voltage, which is a force that moves electrical current. The current moves through wires made of metals called conductors. The wires carry the current to whatever part needs electricity, such as the light bulb in a flashlight. The most common metals used in wires are copper and aluminum, because they're good conductors of electricity.

CHAPTER NINE

STATIC ELECTRICITY

Electric current isn't the only form electricity can take. Another form of electricity is static electricity. This is a buildup of opposite electric charges on objects. These charges are static, or at rest. They can't move away. These charges will build up until they can move away. They may do this through an electric current or a static discharge, or shock.

If you've ever walked across a carpet in your socks and then touched a metal doorknob, the shock you felt was a static discharge. The motion of your socks on the carpet created an imbalance in the electrical charge of your body. When you touched the metal doorknob, the imbalance equalized, creating the electric shock you felt.

One common example of an electrical discharge is lightning. When there's an imbalance of electrical charges in the clouds, the charges try to equalize by passing between the clouds and the ground. This creates lightning bolts.

CHAPTER TEN

ATTRACT AND REPEL

The other part of the electromagnetic force is magnetism. Magnetism is the result of the force that magnetic fields **exert** on charged particles. Magnets can either attract or repel other objects. All matter experiences magnetism, but some materials, like iron, experience it more strongly than others.

Magnets have two poles, a north pole and a south pole. Like the charged particles found inside an atom, the poles of a magnet can either attract or repel each other. The opposite poles of a magnet attract each other, while like poles repel. If you place two magnets on a table and try to move the two north poles together, they will repel each other. If you turn one of the magnets around, you can feel the north and south poles attracting each other.

Magnets always have a north pole and a south pole. Even if you were to cut these magnets in half, they would still have ends that repel and ends that attract.

CHAPTER ELEVEN

WHAT IS A MAGNETIC FIELD?

If you put a magnet and an iron nail at separate ends of a table and slowly move the magnet toward the nail, the nail will eventually move across the table and stick to the magnet. This may look like a magic trick, but it isn't magic. It's science.

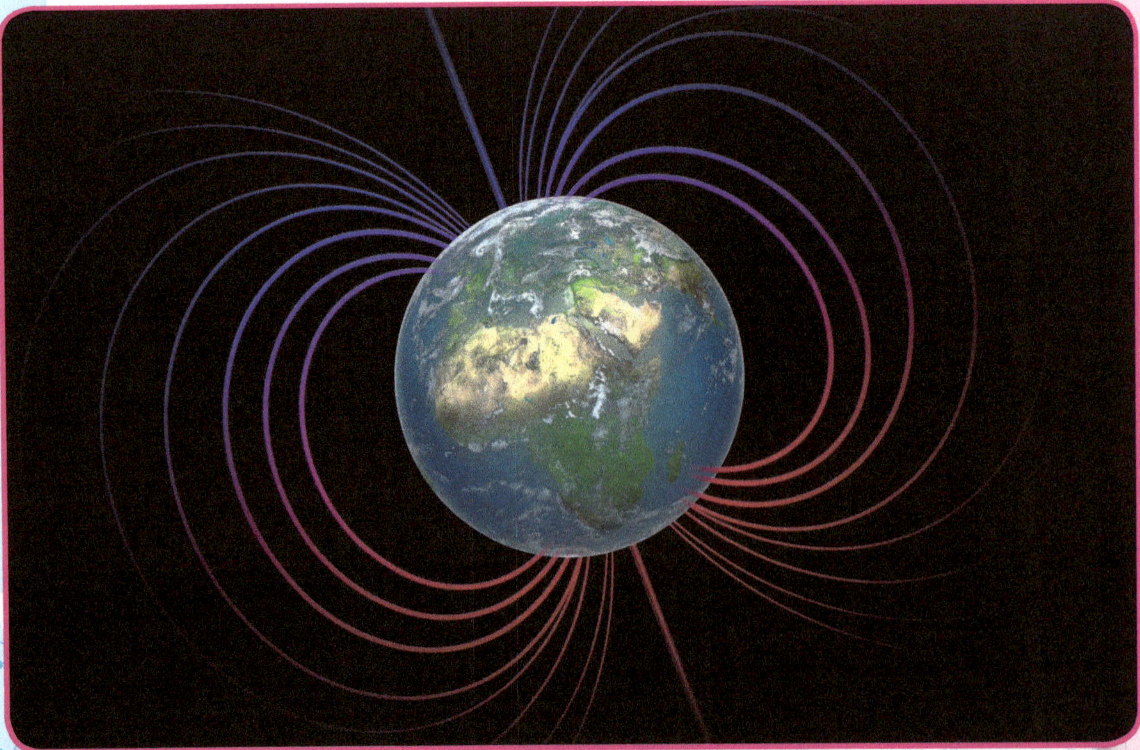

Most of Earth's magnetic field is generated by forces inside the planet. The area of space dominated by its magnetic field is called the magnetosphere.

The reason the nail moves toward the magnet is because of the magnet's magnetic field. A magnetic field is an invisible area that extends around the magnet in which its magnetic forces affect other objects. This field allows the magnet to attract or repel nearby objects. The force a magnet's magnetic field exerts on an object gets weaker the farther it is from that object. In the example above, the magnet didn't attract the nail until the magnet was close enough for the magnetic field to affect it.

CHAPTER TWELVE

USING MAGNETIC FORCES

Magnets can be fun to play with, but they also have many important uses. The earliest known use of magnetism is the compass. Compasses use magnetized needles to indicate which direction is north. They have been used in navigation for hundreds of years. The earliest compasses were used by the Chinese in the 11th century.

Magnets are important components in electric motors, which can be found in most kitchen appliances, fans, and power tools. Electricity generates a magnetic field in wire coils, and this field pushes against the magnetic field generated by a fixed magnet. The push and pull of these two magnetic fields makes part of the motor spin at high speeds. Magnets also help read and write data on your computer's hard drive. Magnetic fields are also used in magnetic resonance imaging, or MRI, which allows doctors to generate images of their patients' organs.

The images produced by the magnetic fields of an MRI machine help doctors diagnose and treat their patients.

CHAPTER THIRTEEN

MAY THE FORCES BE WITH YOU

Humans were interested in the world around them long before modern science could explain how the world works. Ancient peoples studied the natural world for a number of reasons, from predicting the weather to discovering which plants can be used as medicine.

People long ago knew about electricity by experiencing lightning. They knew an object would fall towards the ground if it was dropped. Today, we know that gravity, electricity, and magnetism are forces that influence the world around us at all times. Understanding how these fundamental forces work has given scientists a better understanding of the universe. Some scientists believe all four fundamental forces may be part of a single, unified force. However, no one has been able to prove that theory—yet. Imagine what scientists could learn about these forces in the future.

GLOSSARY

component (kuhm-POH-nuhnt) One of the parts of something.

distort (dih-STOHRT) Altered from a true, natural, or normal state, shape, or condition.

emit (EE-miht) To give off.

exert (ihg-ZUHRT) To put forth effort.

fundamental (fuhn-duh-MEHN-tuhl) Forming or related to one of the basic and important parts of something.

negative (neh-guh-TIV) Having more electrons than protons.

neutral (NOO-truhl) Without an electrical charge.

particle (PAHR-tih-kuhl) A very small piece of something.

physicist (FIH-zuh-sihst) A person who studies physics, or the science that deals with matter and energy and their interactions.

repel (rih-PEHL) To force something to move away or apart.

space-time (SPAYS-tym) A system of one temporal, or time-related, and three spatial, or space-related, coordinates by which any physical object or event can be located.

INDEX

PRIMARY SOURCE LIST

Page 9
Philosophiae Naturalis Principia Mathematica. Book. 1687. Sir Isaac Newton. Wren Library, Trinity College, Cambridge, England.

Page 10
Albert Einstein. Photograph. 1930. Taken in Cuba. Held by Getty Images.

Page 19
Charles-Augustin de Coulomb. Oil on canvas. 1894. Louis Hierle. Palace of Versailles Collection, Versailles.

WEBSITES

Due to the changing nature of Internet links, PowerKids Press has developed an online list of websites related to the subject of this book. This site is updated regularly. Please use this link to access the list: www.powerkidslinks.com/SOPS/gravmagelectric